DISNEY
MULAN

Adaptation by Stevie Stack
Translation by Tom Wang
Illustrated by the Disney Storybook Art Team

BuzzPoP

BuzzPop

An imprint of Little Bee Books
251 Park Avenue South, New York, NY 10010
Copyright © 2019 Disney Enterprises, Inc.

BuzzPop and associated colophon are trademarks
of Little Bee Books.
Manufactured in China TPL 1219
First Edition
10 9 8 7 6 5 4 3 2 1
ISBN 978-1-4998-0951-0
buzzpopbooks.com
For more information about special discounts on
bulk purchases, please contact Little Bee Books
at sales@littlebeebooks.com.

很多年以前，在中国有一位年轻的**姑娘**叫木兰，她准备去见镇上的媒婆.

Hěn duō nián yǐ qián, zài zhōng guó yǒu yí wèi nián qīng de **gū niang** jiào mù lán, tā zhǔn bèi qù jiàn zhèn shàng de méi pó.

Many years ago in China, a young **woman** named Mulan was preparing to meet the town Matchmaker.

可是媒婆见了木兰却断言说她永远不会给自己的家族**增光**.

Kě shì méi pó jiàn le mù lán què duàn yán shuō tā yǒng yuǎn bú huì gěi zì jǐ de jiā zú **zēng guāng**.

But Mulan did not impress the Matchmaker, who told her that she would never bring **honor** to her family.

木兰感到非常**羞愧**, 因为她最希望的就是荣耀自己的家族.

Mù lán gǎn dào fēi cháng **xiū kuì**, yīn wèi tā zuì xī wàng de jiù shì róng yào zì jǐ de jiā zú.

Mulan was filled with **shame** because she wanted more than anything to honor her family.

匈奴单于带**兵**来犯中国长城，皇帝决定派兵反击.

Xiōng nú chán yú dài bīng lái fàn zhōng guó cháng chéng, huáng dì jué dìng pài bīng fǎn jī.

When the warrior Shan-Yu and his Hun **army** attacked the Great Wall of China, the Emperor decided to assemble an army to fight back.

木兰的父亲被征召入伍，可是他体弱无**力**，无法打仗.

Mù lán de fù qin bèi zhēng zhào rù wǔ, kě shì tā tǐ ruò wú **lì**, wú fǎ dǎ zhàng.

Mulan's father was called to join the army, but he was not **strong** enough to fight.

于是木兰把自己乔装成一个**小伙子**, 替父从军.

Yú shì Mù lán bǎ zì jǐ qiáo zhuāng chéng yí ge **xiǎo huǒ zi**, tì fù cóng jūn.

Mulan disguised herself as a **man** to take her father's place in the army.

木兰穿上父亲的盔甲, 跨上战马, 连**夜**驰骋而去.

Mù lán chuān shàng fù qin de kuī jiǎ, kuà shàng zhàn mǎ, lián **yè** chí chěng ér qù.

She put on her father's armor and left at **night** on horseback.

木兰的祖先们为了帮助和**保护**木兰，给她派去了小龙木须.

Mù lán de zǔ xiān men wèi le bāng zhù hé bǎo hù mù lán, gěi tā pài qù le xiǎo lóng mù xū.

Mulan's Ancestors sent Mushu, a small dragon, to help and **protect** Mulan.

木须在**军营**外面找到了木兰.

Mù xū zài **jūn yíng** wài mian zhǎo dào le mù lán.

Mushu found Mulan outside of the army **camp**.

木兰进入军营报到时，遇到了负责训练新兵的商**队长**.

Mù lán jìn rù jūn yíng bào dào shí, yù dào le fù zé xùn liàn xīn bīng de shāng **duì zhǎng**.

When Mulan entered the camp, she met Shang, the **captain** in charge of training the new recruits.

为了准备好上战场，木兰和她的战友们**练兵**数日.

Wèi le zhǔn bèi hǎo shàng zhàn chǎng, Mù lán hé tā de zhàn yǒu men **liàn bīng** shù rì.

It took many days of **training** for Mulan and her fellow recruits to learn how to fight.

终于，他们准备**出征**了.

Zhōng yú, tā men zhǔn bèi **chū zhēng** le.

But eventually, they were ready to head out into **battle**.

商队长带着**部队**穿越乡村，却看到很多的中国军队都被匈奴打败了。

Shāng duì zhǎng dài zhe bù duì chuān yuè xiāng cūn, què kàn dào hěn duō de zhōng guó jūn duì dōu bèi xiōng nú dǎ bài le.

Shang led his **troops** across the countryside, but he found that all of the other troops and villagers they encountered had been defeated by the Huns.

匈奴人发现了商的部队，开始**进攻**。 但木兰引发了雪崩，埋葬了匈奴大军.

Xiōng nú rén fā xiàn le shāng de bù duì, kāi shǐ jìn gōng. Dàn mù lán yǐn fā le xuě bēng, mái zàng le xiōng nú dà jūn.

The Huns found and **attacked** Shang's troops, but Mulan caused an avalanche that buried all the Huns.

雪浪险些把商冲下悬崖，幸亏木兰及时出手相救.

Xuě làng xiǎn xiē bǎ shāng chōng xià xuán yá, xìng kuī mù lán jí shí chū shǒu xiāng jiù.

She then rescued Shang, catching him before the **snow** swept him over a cliff.

商**发现**木兰原来是个女孩儿，便丢下木兰，带着队伍离开了.

Shāng fā xiàn mù lán yuán lái shì gè nǚ háir, biàn diū xià mù lán, dài zhe duì wu lí kāi le.

Shang **discovered** that Mulan was actually a woman, and he and his troops left without her.

但是木兰得知单于和一些匈奴兵还**活着**，于是赶去警告商.

Dàn shì Mù lán dé zhī chán yú hé yì xiē xiōng nú bīng hái **huó zhe**, yú shì gǎn qù jǐng gào shāng.

But Mulan learned that Shan-Yu and some of the Huns were still **alive**, so she raced off to warn Shang.

在都城内，木兰把她的战友们改扮成妇女，混入并保卫**皇宫**.

Zài dū chéng nèi, mù lán bǎ tā de zhàn yǒu men gǎi bàn chéng fù nǚ, hùn rù bìng bǎo wèi **huáng gōng**.

In the Imperial City, Mulan disguised her fellow recruits as women so they could sneak into the **palace** and defend it from the Hun soldiers.

木兰把单于困在了**屋顶**，木须用火箭猛击单于.

Mù lán bǎ chán yú kùn zài le wū dǐng, mù xū yòng huǒ jiàn měng jī chán yú.

Mulan trapped Shan-Yu on the **roof**, and Mushu crashed into him with a rocket.

火光四射，宣示着木兰和她的朋友们最终打败了匈奴单于。

Huǒ guāng sì shè, xuān shì zhe mù lán hé tā de péng you men zuì zhōng dǎ bài le xiōng nú chán yú.

Fireworks exploded, signaling that Mulan and her friends had finally defeated Shan-Yu and the Huns.

每一个人，包括皇上都向木兰鞠躬**致谢**！

Měi yí ge rén, bāo kuò huáng shang dōu xiàng mù lán jū gōng **zhì xiè**!

Everyone **thanked** and bowed to Mulan, including the Emperor!

木兰的**英勇**光耀了门庭.

Mù lán de yīng yǒng guāng yào le mén tíng.

Mulan's **bravery** brought honor to her family.